I'M GOING TO THE OCEAN!

I'M GOING

TO THE OCEAN!

BY ELEANOR SCHICK

THE MACMILLAN COMPANY, New York · COLLIER-MACMILLAN LIMITED, London

The Macmillan Company, New York
Collier-Macmillan Canada, Ltd., Toronto, Ontario
Library of Congress catalog card number: 66-17903

Printed in the United States of America
FIRST PRINTING

For Jack

Robin was sitting by the river one day with his dog Domino, talking to his friends the fish.

All of a sudden a large bird appeared

and stopped to drink.

"Where do you come from?" Robin asked.

"I come from the ocean," the bird replied. "I am a sea gull."

"Our grandparents told us about the ocean," said the fish.

"I would like to see the ocean," said Robin.
"Then follow me," said the sea gull, "and I will take you there!"

So Robin left, with Domino following close behind him.

On their way they passed some horses grazing in a meadow.

And some swans feeding on a lake.

They stopped in a barnyard to rest a minute. "I'm going to see the ocean," Robin whispered to the hens.

And Domino told the baby chicks.

"I'm going to see the ocean," Robin said to the deer

as they passed through the woods.

"I'm going to see the ocean," he called to the rabbits

as he crossed an open field.

"I'm going to the ocean!" he sang to the mice

as he galloped over the sun-warmed rocks.

"Hey, butterflies, I'm going to the ocean!" he cried out

as he leaped across the prickly grasses.

"I'm going to the ocean!" he said over and over to himself
as he ran across the sand up onto a high dune.

And as the sea gull swooped down
to meet his friends, Robin shouted—

"The ocean!"

And he and Domino sat and looked for a long, long time.